Animal Antics
A to Z

PRESENTED BY

Anita Lobel

Greenwillow Books
An Imprint of HarperCollins*Publishers*

Animal Antics: From A to Z

Copyright © 2005 by Anita Lobel

All rights reserved. Manufactured in China.

www.harperchildrens.com

Watercolor paints and white gouache were used to prepare the full-color art.
The text type is 32-point Windsor.

Library of Congress Cataloging-in-Publication Data
Lobel, Anita.
Animal antics: from a to z / by Anita Lobel.
p. cm.
"Greenwillow Books."
ISBN 0-06-051814-6 (trade). ISBN 0-06-051815-4 (lib. bdg.)
1. Circus—Juvenile Literature. 2. English language—Alphabet—Juvenile Literature.
I. Title.
GV1817.L63 2005 791.3—dc22 2004042536

First Edition 10 9 8 7 6 5 4 3 2 1

Greenwillow Books

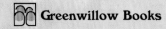

illy,
for you, again and always

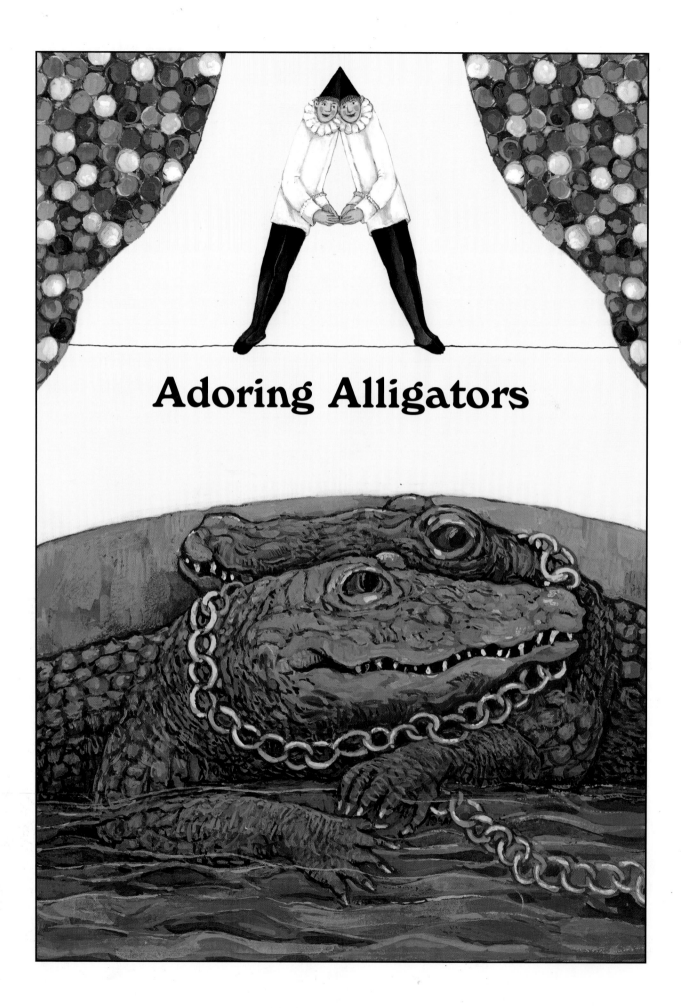

Adoring Alligators

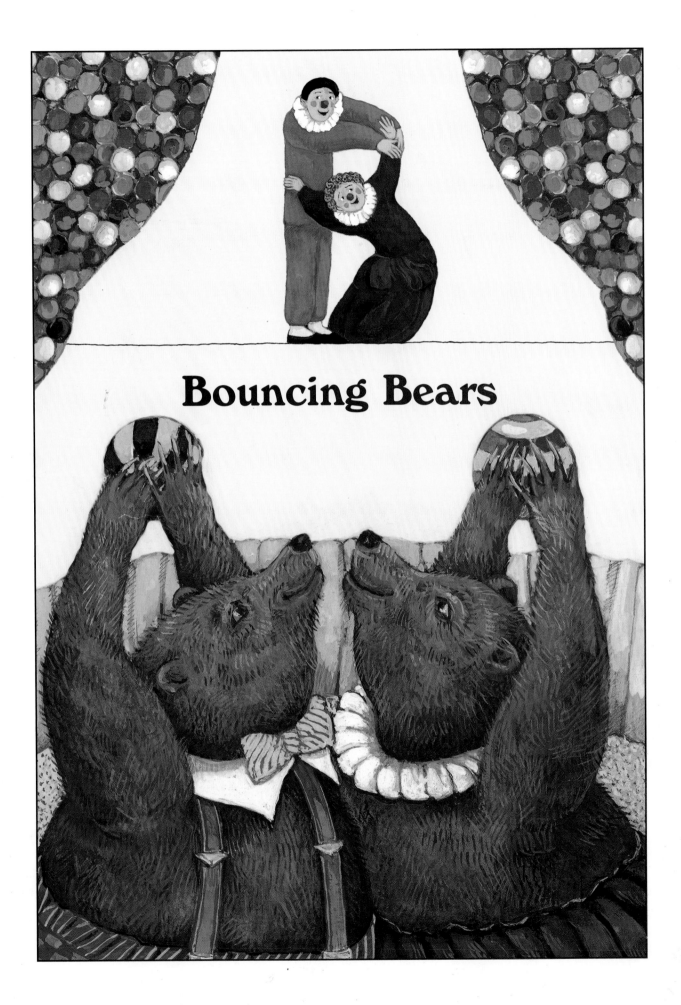

Bouncing Bears

Charming Camels

Dainty Deer

Elated Elephants

Fanciful Foxes

Glamorous
Giraffes

Happy Hippopotamuses

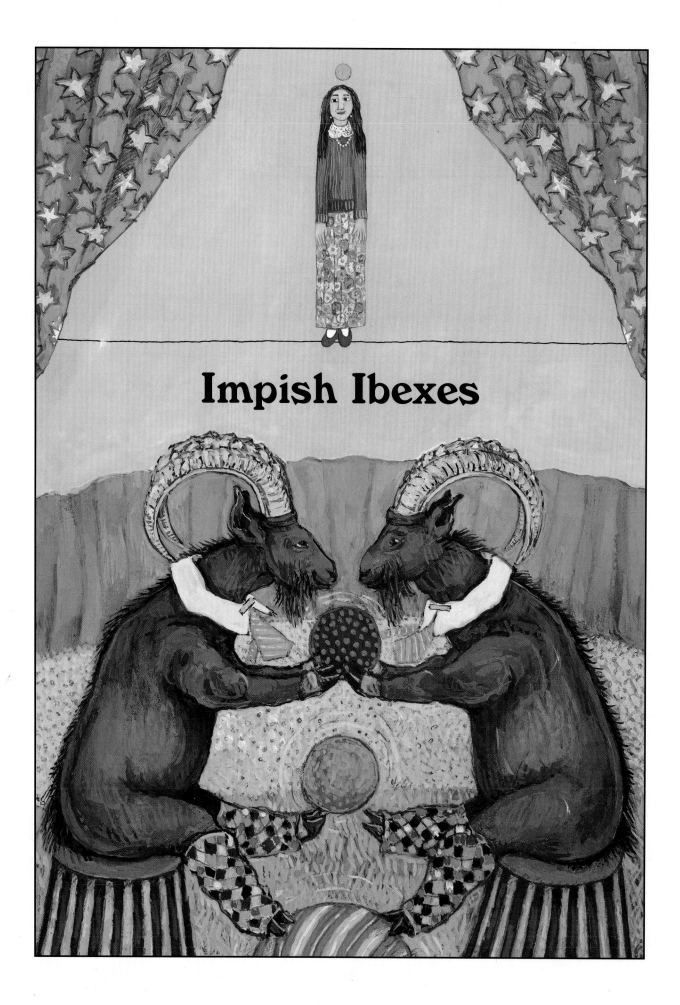

Impish Ibexes

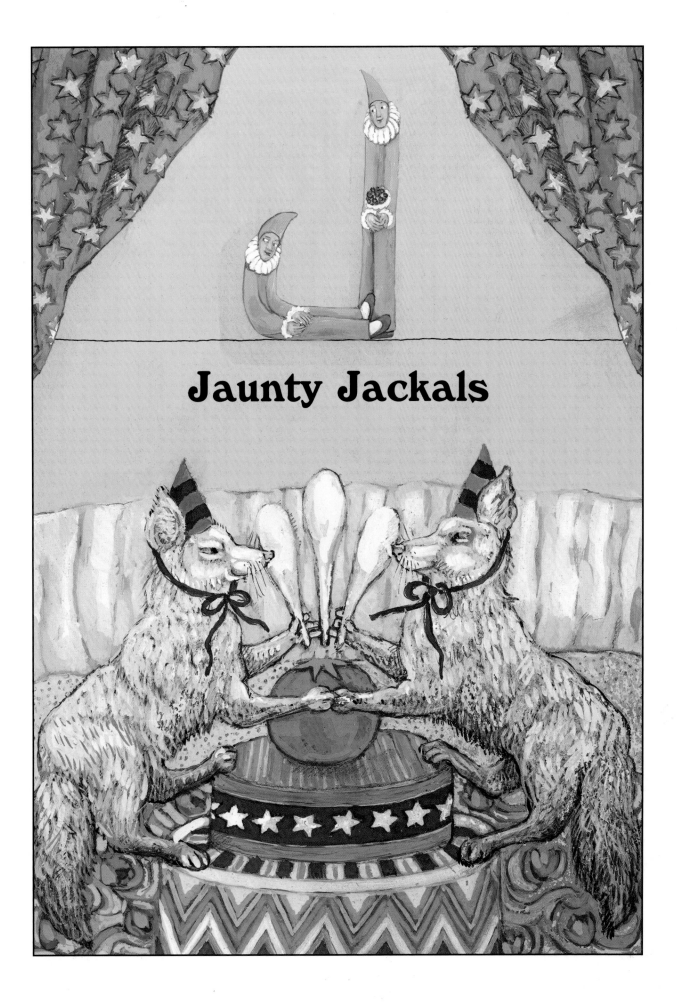

Jaunty Jackals

Kooky Koalas

Lovable Lions

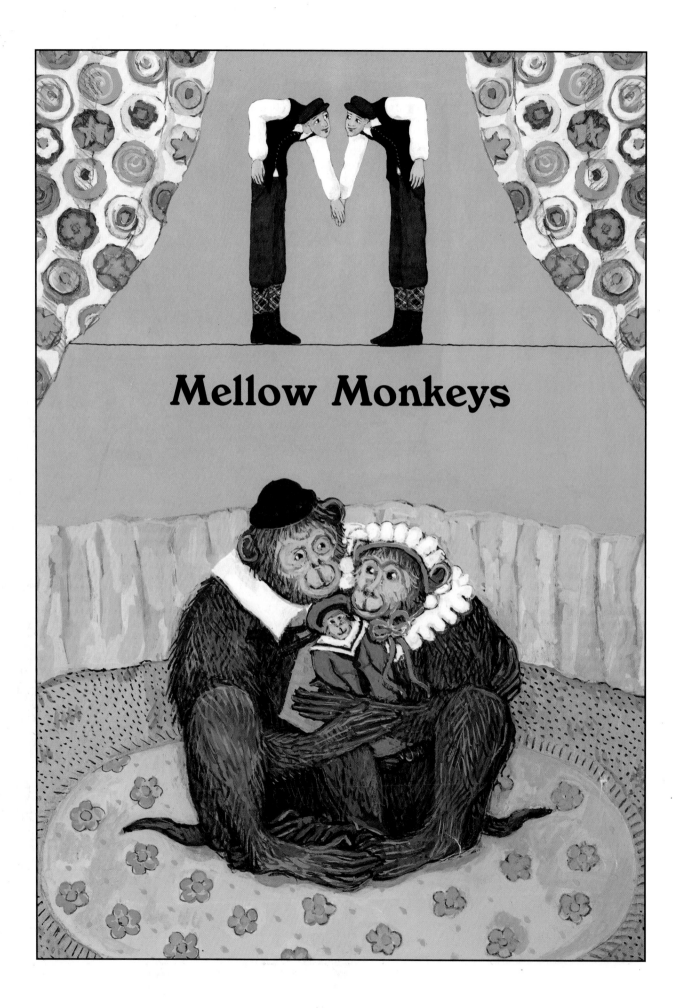

Mellow Monkeys

Nice Nyalas

Obedient Ostriches

Playful Pigs

Quaint
Quetzals

Romping Rabbits

Silly Seals

Tender Tigers

Unlikely Unicorns

Vigorous Vultures

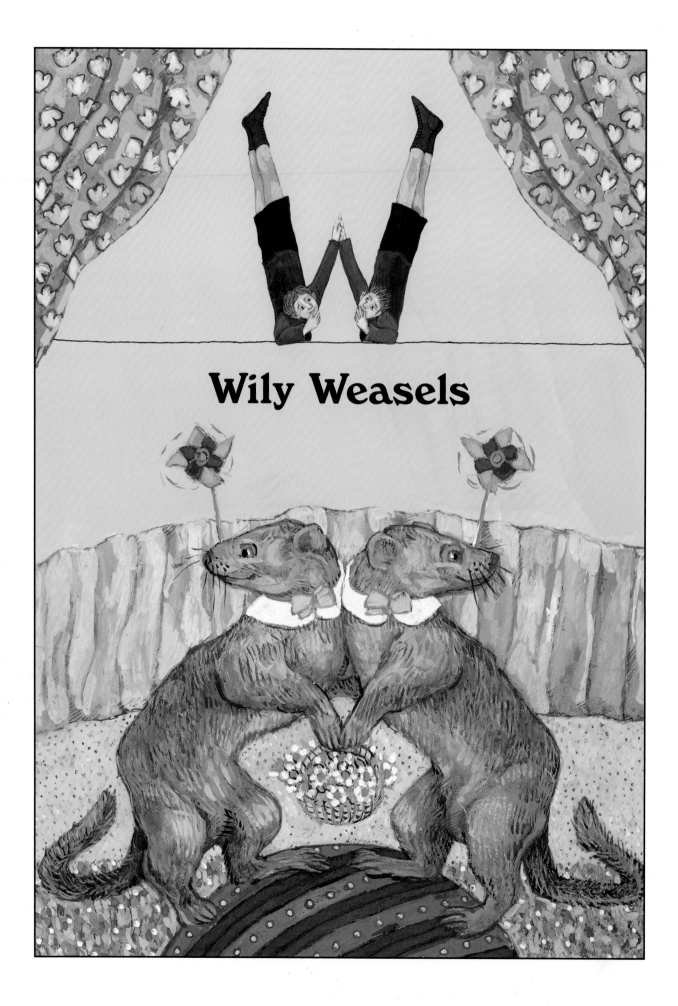

Wily Weasels

eXuberant Xenopus

Yoked Yaks

Zany Zebras

Animal Answers

Alligators live in swampy areas where rivers flow, such as in the Florida Everglades, the Gulf Coast, and the Yangtze River Valley in China. Their teeth are sharp weapons. They are smooth swimmers but are clumsy on land.

Bears live in the mountains and forests of North America and in many regions of Europe and Asia. Almost all bears are good at swimming and climbing trees. They eat many different kinds of food, including fruits, plants, fish, and small animals.

Camels live in the deserts of Asia and northern Africa, where they are useful carriers of people and goods. When food is scarce, they can live on fat stored in their humps and can go without water for several days. The camel is sometimes called "the ship of the desert."

Deer are plentiful in forests and mountains almost everywhere in the world. There are many different kinds of deer. Reindeer are one kind, and they are famous for pulling Santa's sled at Christmastime.

Elephants live in Africa and Asia. They are loyal to their herds and families and are very smart. Some elephants have even been taught by humans to paint!

Foxes are smart and sneaky hunters who mostly live in the forests and mountains of North America, Asia, and Europe. They usually have silvery gray or red fur and long bushy tails. Foxes are standard characters in folk and fairy tales.

Giraffes live in herds on the African plains. They are peaceful and elegant vegetarians, who feed on leaves from the tops of trees.

Hippopotamuses live in watery riverbeds in Africa. They stay with their families and herds, spending most of their time in the water. The word "hippopotamus" means "river horse" in Greek.

Ibexes are a type of goat. They are great climbers, inhabiting very high mountains in central Asia, southern Europe, and northeastern Africa. They are distinguished by their elaborate horns.

Jackals are in the dog family. On the African and Asian deserts and plains, they run in pairs or in small packs. Jackals hunt small animals and scavenge for plants. They do not usually attack animals larger than they are.

Koalas are native to Australia. They are accomplished climbers who live in eucalyptus trees and eat their leaves.

Lions are among the largest cats. They now live and hunt mostly in the grassy plains and sparsely forested lowlands and hills of central Africa. If they don't feel threatened, they are not dangerous to humans.

Monkeys come in many varieties and sizes. They are plentiful in the jungles of Africa, Asia, and South America. They are smart and social animals.

Nyalas are a graceful species of antelope from southeastern Africa. The males tend to be gray-brown and the females a reddish mahogany color.

Ostriches are native to the grasslands and semideserts of Africa, but they can also be found on farms or ranches throughout the world. They are cumbersome, heavy, "walking" birds that do not fly. At one time ostrich feathers were prized decorations in ladies' hats.

Pigs are charming and smart and like to roll around in mud. They are useful farm animals everywhere in the world. Some kinds of pigs are even kept as pets.

Quetzals are striking, colorful tropical jungle birds. They come from South and Central America. Feathers from their long tails were valuable to tribal chiefs.

Rabbits come in many different colors and varieties. In the wild they live in forests and deserts all over the world. When domesticated, they are valued farm animals and delightful pets.

Seals live in large numbers in the seas and coastal areas of the north Atlantic and Pacific. They feed on small fish, crabs, and other ocean creatures. Some seals can bend so far backward that they can touch their back flippers with their noses.

Tigers are great beautiful cats that live in the forests of Asia. In northern parts of the continent, they live in Siberia. Farther south they are found in India and China. Tigers enjoy swimming, but they do not like climbing trees.

Unicorns are mythic creatures that exist only in stories. They look like horses with a single horn growing from the middle of the forehead. If you strap a cone onto the head of a pony, you can pretend that he is one of the unicorns in my circus.

Vultures are large majestic birds. They scavenge for remnants of dead animals in the forests and plains of North and South America, southern Europe, northern Africa, and central Asia.

Weasels are found in Europe, Asia, Africa, and North America. They are small courageous hunters both by day and night. Weasels are great climbers and fast runners. If they are frightened or cornered, they spray a bad-smelling fluid for protection.

Xenopus are African clawed frogs. Their claws, as well as their flattened bodies, make them well suited to life under water.

Yaks are useful, huge animals related to oxen. They can be found in Tibet and northeastern China, both in the wild and on farms. Domestic yaks are used for transport, they provide milk, and their droppings are often used as fuel.

Zebras are elegant and peaceful animals. They live and graze in large herds in many parts of Africa. Zebras have a keen sense of hearing, and they are sensitive to the smell of smoke.

—Anita Lobel